CH00859138

Jittery Jenny

BY Jamie Sussel Turner

ILLUSTRATED BY Madonna Davidoff

Published by Less Stress Publishing
www.lessstresscoach.com

GIRL FRIDAY
PRODUCTIONS®

Edited and designed by
Girl Friday Productions
www.girlfridayproductions.com

Design: Paul Barrett
Book development and
   project management: Sara Spees Addicott
Editorial: Dave Valencia

ISBN (paperback): 978-1-7335074-2-4
ISBN (hardcover): 978-1-7335074-1-7
Library of Congress
   Control Number: 2021912162

To my grandchildren: Jillian, Amy, Maeve, Niko, and Cal

—JST

To my grandsons Luca and Roman

—MD

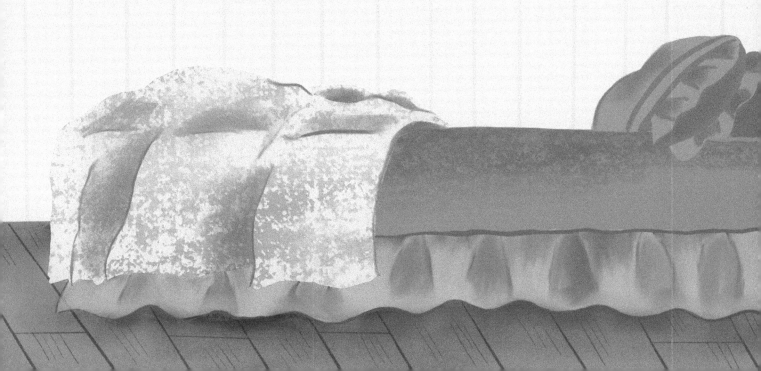

"Time to wake up," shouted Mama.
"Second grade is here!"
    Jenny hugged her blanket. Her
stomach felt jumpy.

She worried, I'm not ready for second grade. First grade was fun. I was the best reader in my class. But what if my new teacher doesn't like me?

It wasn't even breakfast time, and her little sister, Amy, was at it again, doing back walkovers all over the house.

That looks too scary for me to even try,
Jenny thought.

Mama took a first-day-of-school picture.
Jenny's smile shivered.

Jenny strolled to school and worried, *What if I can't find a friend to play with at recess?*

Some boys spotted Jenny alone, rocking side to side, biting her lip. They yelled, "Jittery Jenny, Jittery Jenny!"

Jenny wished she were invisible.

The next week, Jenny's first math test came back covered in red circles with a note from Ms. Ward that said, "Jenny, see me on Monday."

Oh no, oh no, oh no. This is terrible! I've never had to see the teacher, Jenny thought.

On her walk home, Jenny worried that Mama and Papa would ask about her test. She raced inside and shoved the paper under her pillow.

After Mama tucked Jenny in bed and headed downstairs, Jenny slithered the test out from its hiding place. She stared and stared at Ms. Ward's note. *Boy, I'm in big trouble*, Jenny thought.

On Sunday, Grandpa took Jenny to the beach.

Other kids were splashing and laughing, but Jenny nibbled her nails as she imagined a huge wave spinning her away from Grandpa's grasp.

Grandpa said, "Jenny, I know the ocean can feel scary. No one can control the ocean waves. They will keep coming and coming. But you can be Zen about the ocean."

"What do you mean, Grandpa?" Jenny said.

"Well," Grandpa said, "if you're worried about going in the ocean, you can be the boss of your brain and come up with some ideas to calm you."

"That boy floating on his back looks pretty calm," Jenny noticed.

"Yes, "Grandpa said. "He's bossing his brain. He's choosing to chill out. A boss has choices. And so do you."

Hmm, what could I do? Jenny thought.

"Maybe I could jump over one of those little waves. Or be braver and go up to my knees," Jenny said.

"It's up to you, Jenny," Grandpa said. "When you get the hang of bossing your brain, you won't feel so jittery."

Jenny grabbed Grandpa's hand and inched to the edge of the
water. She took a few tiny steps as the ocean tickled her toes.
Squeezing Grandpa's hand tighter, Jenny spotted a just-
right wave and jumped. "Whoo-hoo!" she shouted.

The next morning, Jenny looked at Ms. Ward's note again. And instead of moaning, *Oh no, oh no, oh no,* she wondered, *How could I be the boss of these brain jitters?*

At breakfast Jenny handed Mama the test and stammered, "I'm sorry for not showing you this sooner, Mama. But, I have a plan. I could ask Ms. Ward to take the test again, or I could think; *It's just the first test. Ms. Ward will help me do better on the next one.*"

"So what will you do?" Mama asked.
"I'll try to talk to Ms. Ward about doing better."

Talking to Mama wasn't hard. Maybe talking to Ms. Ward won't be either, Jenny thought.

On her way to school that morning, instead of going, *Oh no, oh no, oh no,* Jenny thought about talking with Ms. Ward, took a deep breath, and went, *"Aahhhh."*

Check your work,
don't rush,
ask for help.

Ms. Ward gave Jenny a few tips and didn't yell at her at all. *Whew, that wasn't so bad,* thought Jenny.

But as Jenny headed out to recess she spotted those mean boys again. *Think quick, how can I boss my brain right now?* she wondered.

Two ideas popped up. *I could stomp past the boys, or I could tell them to stop.*

As Jenny ran to meet her friends, the mean boys chanted, "Jittery Jenny, Jittery Jenny." Jenny slammed on her brakes and looked those boys right in their eyes and said . . .

"You've got it wrong. I'm not Jittery Jenny.
From now on I'm **Zen Jen**."

A Note to Parents, Caregivers, Teachers, and School Counselors

Jittery Jenny was inspired by my granddaughter during a conversation in the fall of 2020 during the COVID-19 pandemic. She shared how she applied the SURF method from my book *Less Stress Life: How I Went from Crazed to Calm and You Can Too*. When I realized how helpful my method was to calming an eleven-year old, it dawned on me that perhaps I could use my method to help adults to support their anxious kids too.

Overview of SURF Model from *Less Stress Life*

Experienced ocean swimmers know to never turn their backs on the surf. Even a quick nod to friends on the beach can result in injury when an unexpected swell knocks them down and pulls them under.

While staying alert to the surf, ocean swimmers have choices. They can duck under a wave, surf on top of it, plow through it, brace for a hit, or sit it out on the beach.

When you stay alert to your stress you will begin to notice you have choices. You'll learn to recognize and adopt new options so stress doesn't pull you under and hold you in its grip.

Here's an acronym to help you remember the four steps to my Less Stress Life Method:

S: **Spot Your Stress**—catch stress happening in the moment.

U: **Unleash Your Options**—Brainstorm new ways to think and behave.

R: **Respond in a New Way**—Pick one new way and ride out your choice.

F: **Figure Out What Worked**—Reflect on what worked and lock in your new behavior and thinking.

When you follow the four steps in the SURF Method, you and your children will gradually go from crazed to calm. And the payoff is greater clarity, more peace, a presence that invites others to connect with you, and more happiness during each moment of your day—even the ones that aren't going so well.

A no-stress life is not an option—how you choose to respond to stress is!

About the Author

Jamie Sussel Turner, a former school principal, blushed bright red when called on in class and broke out in skin rashes when anxious. Now, with her first picture book, she's on a mission to empower worrying kids to learn to lead calmer lives. **www.lessstresscoach.com**

About the Illustrator

Madonna Davidoff is an Asian American artist who as a young girl dreamt of becoming an architect like her dad, but instead chose to become an illustrator due to the "jitters" she felt during math class. Her dream came true, and she now illustrates children's books. She has lived in the Philippines, Singapore, and Switzerland and is now based in Bucks County, Pennsylvania. **www.madonnadavidoff.com**

Lightning Source UK Ltd.
Milton Keynes UK
UKHW020814131021
392087UK00002B/116

9 781733 507417